THIS COLORING BOOK BELONGS TO:

THIRD MAN RECORDS COLORING BOOK FIRST EDITION
UPDATED 2021

FOR MORE INFORMATION:
THIRD MAN BOOKS, LLC, 623 7TH AVE S, NASHVILLE, TENNESSEE 37203.

ART DIRECTION BY NATHANIO STRIMPOPULOS
ILLUSTRATION BY JOHN SNOW / AGENCYRUSH.COM
DESIGN BY JESSICA YOHN

ISBN 9781734842258

MANNY Lost THE Keys
NSWER IN BACK

Manny AND THE Mandroids
TAP!!
TAP!!

Spot the Difference
prize
Yeah

CAN YOU FIND THE 10 DIFFERENCES
Answers
1. SNAKE HAS A HAT ON
2. 'YEAH' SIGN CHANGES TO 'YEAH MAN!'
3. TOTEM POLE MISSING A WING
4. TROPHY MISSING FROM SHELF
5. FAN MISSING A BLADE
6. MANNY IS NO LONGER PEEKING OVER COUNTER
7. ANOTHER FOOT APPEARS UNDER THE COUNTER
8. SHOPPER HAS ICE CREAM TATTOO
9. FRAME ON RECORD SHELF HAS IMAGE
10. EYE ON RECORD IS CLOSED
prize
Yeah Man!

THIRD MAN PHOTO STUDIO
NASHVILLE
YOUR
HEAR

Lazaretto

the WHITE STRIPES
Airline

The Raconteurs
Broken Boy Soldiers

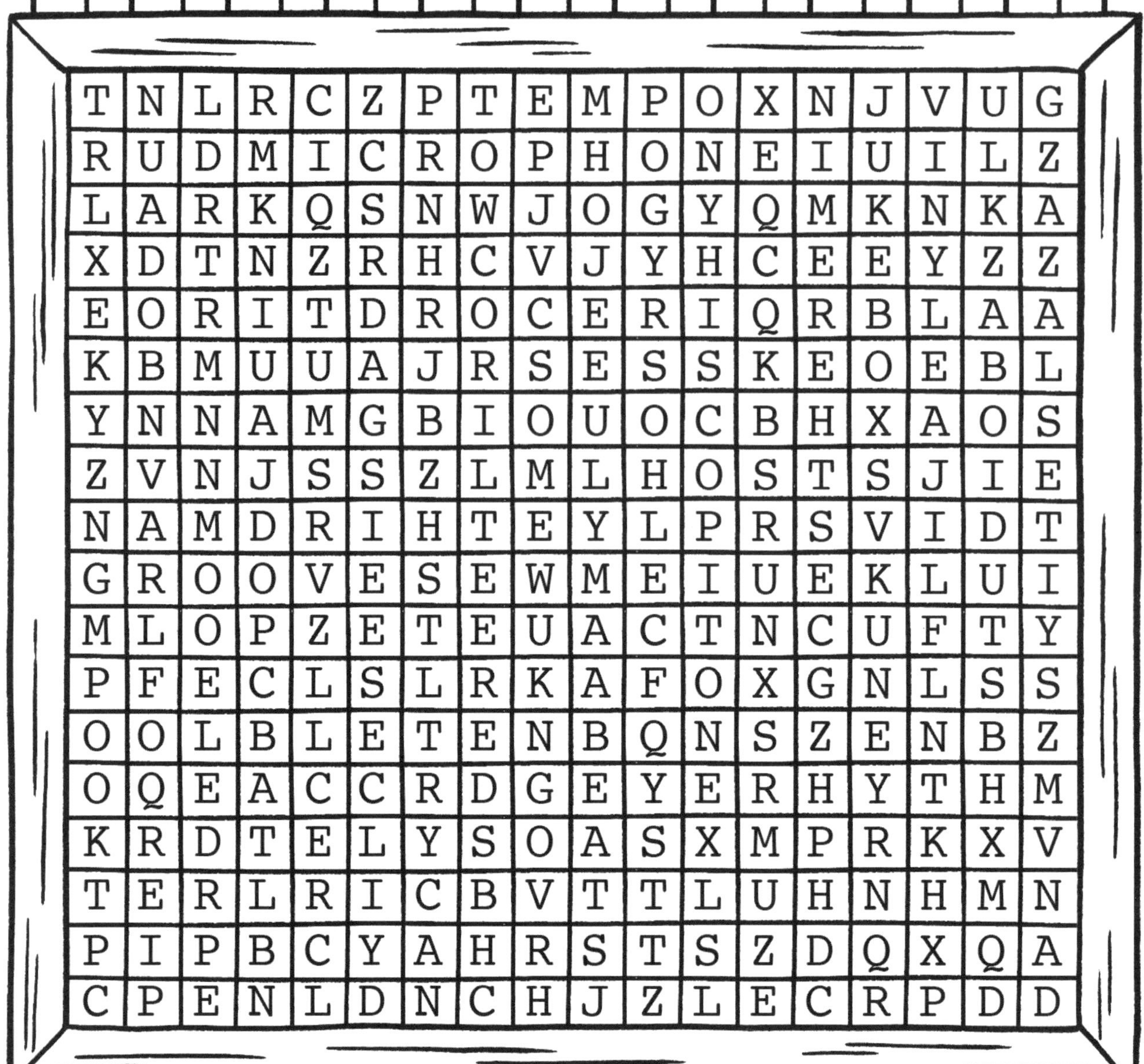

ANSWERS IN BACK

BASS
BEATS
BLUEROOM
CANDY
DRUMS
ELECTRIC
GROOVES
GUITAR
JUKEBOX
MANNY

MICROPHONE
MUSIC
PEDALSTEEL
PLECTRUM
POETRY
RECORD
RHYTHM
ROLLING
RPM
SCOPITONE

SPEAKER
STAGE
STUDIO
TEMPO
TESLA
THEREMIN
THIRDMAN
TREBLE
TURNTABLE
VINYL

CONNECT
THE
Dots

HOT off the PRESS
HOT-N-READY
Vinyl Record

LIGHT
+
SOUND
MACHINE

Match the NAMES to the PICTURES

LISTENING BOOTH
Pick a Song
Manny's TOP TUNES
Pick a Song

NASHVILLE
THIRD MAN RECORDS

ORD STORE DAY

THIRD MAN RECORDS
DETROIT
THE SYNCOPATOR
THIRD MAN RECORDS
441

PHOTO BOOTH
Strike
A POSE

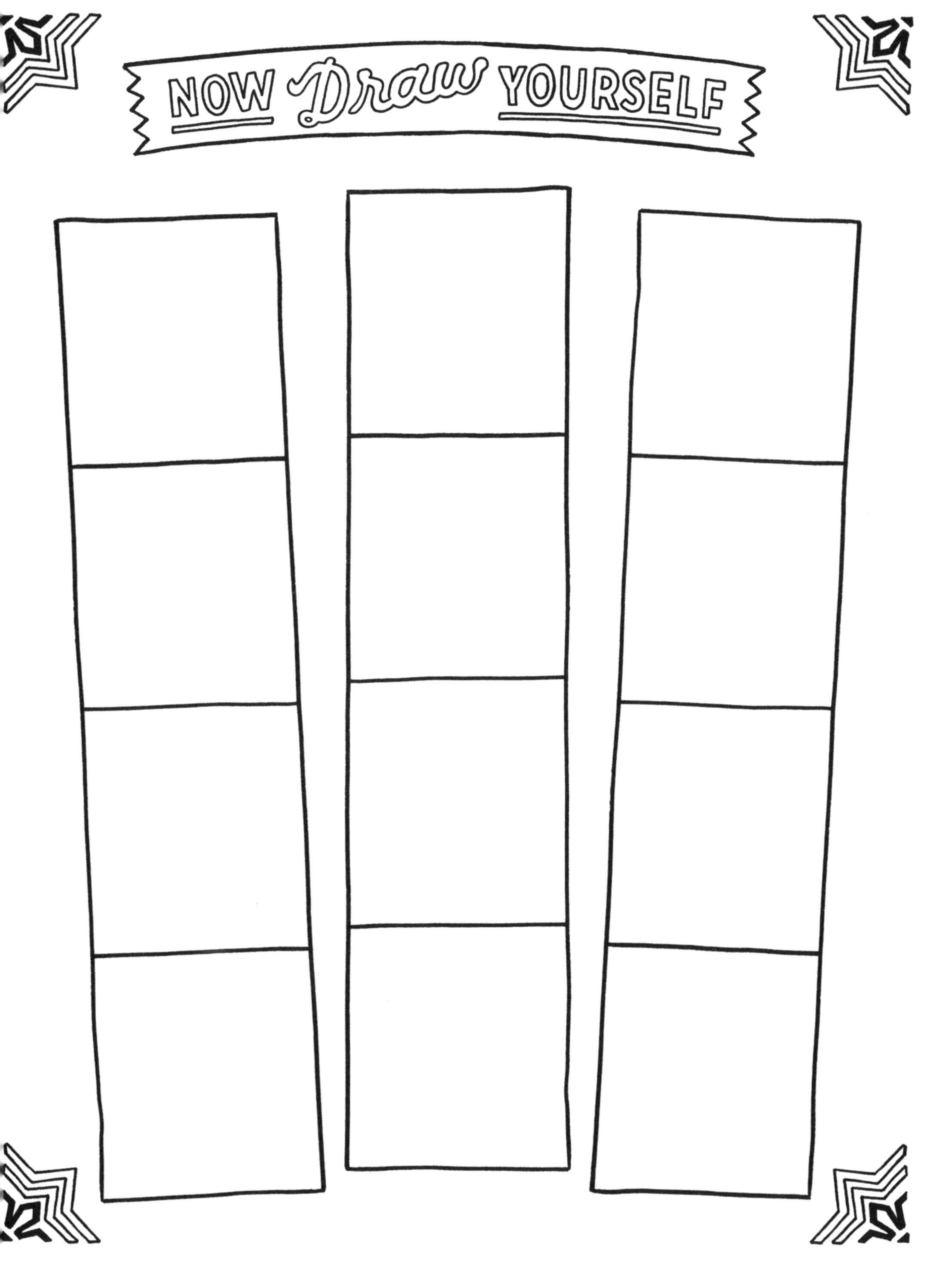
NOW Draw YOURSELF

Monkey Band

MOLD-A-RAMA

Insert your token

The mold is pressed

Your guitar is cast

Claim your prize!

Tic-Tac-Toe

CORN HOLE

THIRD MAN PRESSING
PUCK
PRESS
TRIM

DRAW YOUR OWN
Record Label

THE MUSICIAN PLAYS THEIR MUSIC AND THE SOUND IS RECORDED.

A MASTER DISC IS CUT ON A RECORDING MACHINE CALLED A LATHE.

SKILLED PROFESSIONALS FINELY TUNE THE RECORDING PROCESS.

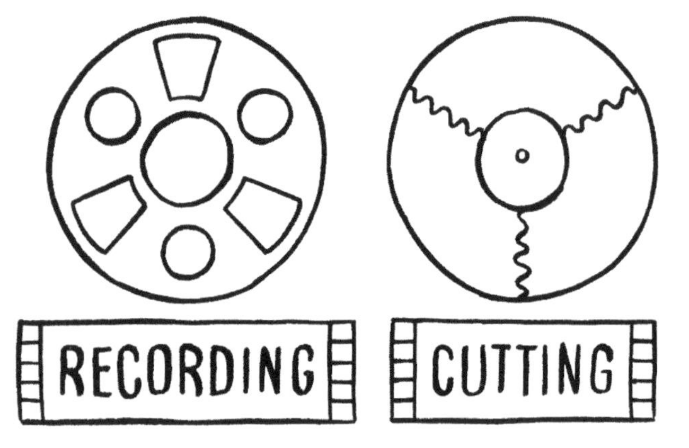

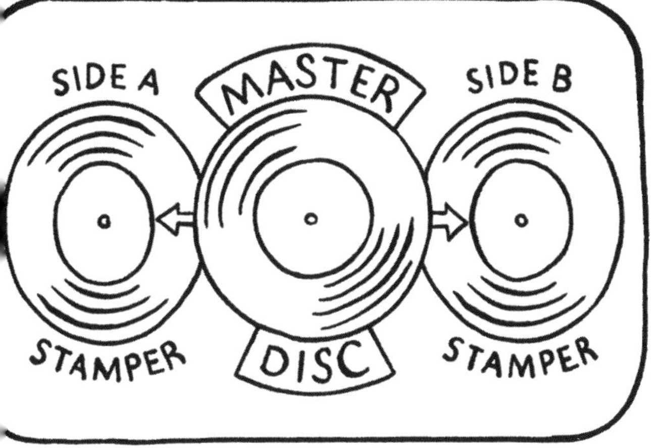

THE MASTER DISC IS USED AS A MOLD TO MAKE STAMPER DISCS.

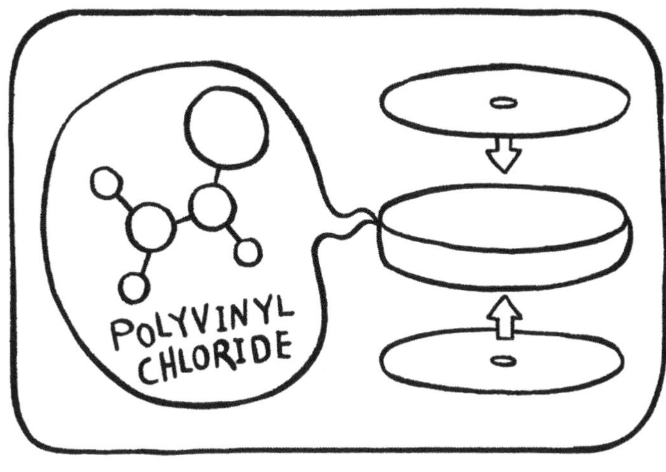

HOT VINYL BISCUITS ARE ARRANGED BETWEEN PRINTED PAPER LABELS.

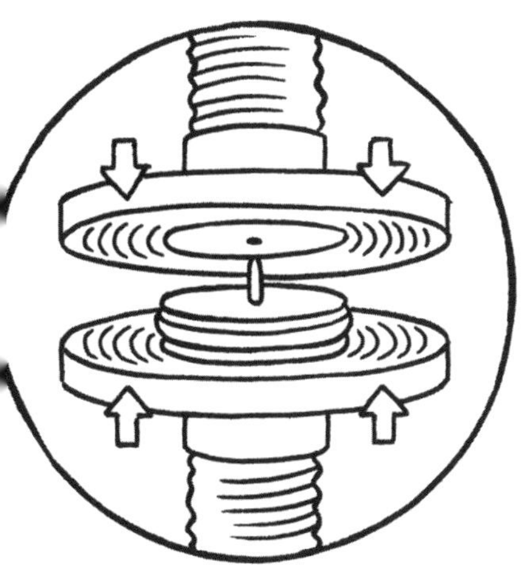

THE VINYL BISCUIT IS READY FOR PRESSING.

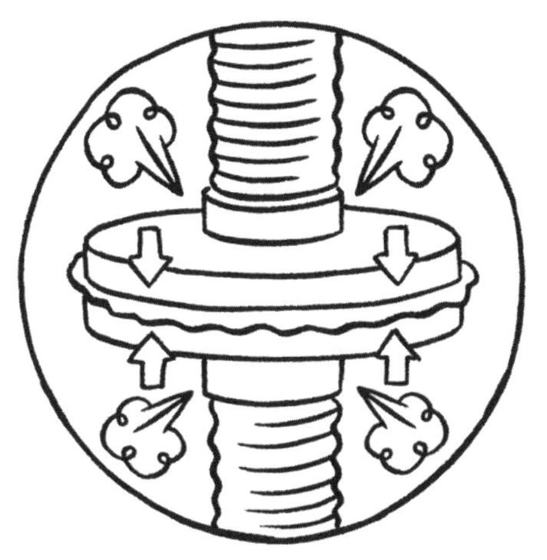

HIGH PRESSURE MAKES THE VINYL EXPAND.

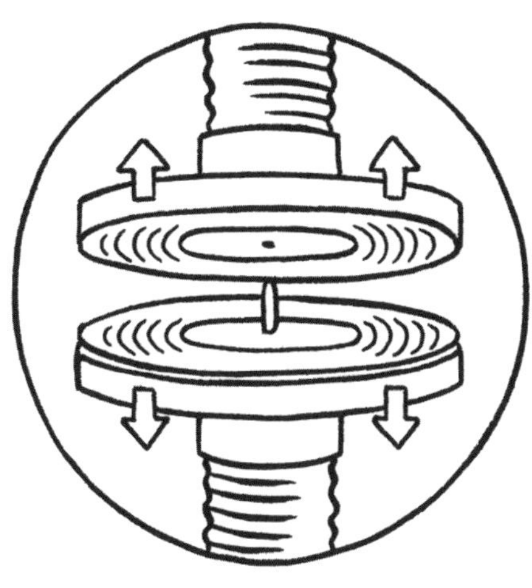

A SHINY NEW RECORD HOT OFF THE PRESS.

FINALLY, THE RECORD IS PACKAGED AND READY TO BE PLAYED.

THIRD MAN BOOKS

ANSWERS FOR WORD SEARCH:

ANSWER FOR MAZE: